The *Supernatural* Quiz Book Season 2

500 questions and answers on *Supernatural* Season 2

By Light Bulb Quizzes

Written by fans, for fans

Unofficial

Published by Light Bulb Quizzes

Edited by

Kim Kimber

www.kimkimber.co.uk

Cover image by

Devin Davis-Lorton

www.devinternet.tumblr.com

All of the questions in this quiz book are based on the DVD
release of *Supernatural* Season 2, produced by Warner Home
Video and the soundtrack and other details may sometimes
vary from that of other versions.

This book is unofficial and unauthorised. All of the questions
have been researched and compiled by Light Bulb Quizzes
who have done their best to ensure that all information is
correct. However, if any sharp-eyed *Supernatural* fans notice
an error, please contact us so that it can be rectified.

For all fans of
Supernatural

Introduction

Following on from *The Supernatural Quiz Book Season 1*, Light Bulb Quizzes has researched and compiled another 500 questions, this time to test your memory of Season 2.

As Dean and Sam Winchester (Jensen Ackles and Jared Padalecki) continue to face up to monsters old and new, from vampires and werewolves to zombies and shapeshifters, our fascination with *Supernatural* is every bit as strong.

Now in Season 10, the show remains as popular as ever with new fans joining old to swell the ratings and increase the *Supernatural* family. Together with our earlier quiz book on Season 1, this book provides background information for those discovering *Supernatural* for the first time and a reminder of *the road so far* for those fans who have loved the show from the outset.

Written and produced by fans of the series for other fans to enjoy, *The Supernatural Quiz Book Season 2* provides you with the opportunity to take another look at past episodes and remember the memorable characters, brought to life by the excellent scripts and talented actors.

As well as questions on all of the individual episodes, we have included sections on many of the Season 2 actors, episode titles, quotes from the series, supporting cast and crew, the soundtrack, monsters and spirits and how to hunt them and much more *Supernatural* trivia.

We hope that you will enjoy the second in our series of quiz books about *Supernatural* as we continue to take a nostalgic look back at the Winchester brothers' epic journey as they follow in the footsteps of their father, John Winchester, carrying on 'the family business'.

Light Bulb Quizzes

Written by fans, for fans

Questions

Episode 1 – In My Time of Dying

1. Which member of the Winchester family is the only one awake in the crashed Impala – John, Dean or Sam?

2. What does Dean find strange about the hospital when he wakes up?

3. What happens when Dean tries to talk to the nurse?

4. What does he discover in a hospital bed?

5. What does the nurse tell Sam about his father, whilst he is in Dean's room?

6. What does the nurse say to Sam about Dean?

7. What does Dean (try to) ask Sam to do?

8. What does John Winchester ask Sam to do?

9. What does Bobby say about the list John Winchester gives to Sam?

10. What does Dean do to let his father and Sam know that he is there – turns on the TV, switches on the light or knocks a glass off the table?

11. What is above his body?

12. Who does Dean meet at the hospital?

13. How does Sam communicate with Dean?

14. Who is Tessa really and why is she talking to Dean?

15. What does John Winchester do to save Dean?

Episode Titles

16. Which episode is named after a 1944 play by Jean-Paul Sartre called *Huis Clos*?

17. Episode 13 'Houses of the Holy' is named after an album by which English rock band?

18. Which episode is named after a book by Kenneth Anger that details scandals of the rich and famous?

19. Episode 8 'Crossroad Blues' is named after a song by which 1930s' American Blues artist?

20. Which episode is named after a song and album by blues singer Albert King?

21. Episode 4 'Children Shouldn't Play With Dead Things' is named after the 1972 movie of the same name – who was the director?

22. Which episode is named after a song that has been recorded by Bob Dylan and Led Zeppelin among others?

23. Episode 2 'Everybody Loves a Clown' shares the same title as a song by which 1960s' American pop and rock band?

24. Which episode is named after a song by country legend Johnny Cash?

25. Episode 3 'Bloodlust' is the name of a book, movie or album?

26. Which episode is named after a 1995 movie starring Kevin Spacey?

27. Episode 9 'Croatoan' takes its name from a word carved in a tree on what island during the 16th century?

28. Which episode is named after a children's game?

29. Episode 20 'What Is and What Should Never Be' is also a song by which band?

30. The title of which two episodes suggests unpredictable, noisy and violent behaviour?

Episode 2 – Everybody Loves a Clown

31. What does the girl see on the way home from the fair?

32. Where does she next see the above?

33. What does it do to the girl's parents?

34. Whose body are Dean and Sam burning at the beginning of the episode?

35. What does Sam find on John Winchester's phone?

36. Where does the address lead the brothers to?

37. What characters are we introduced to in the bar?

38. What does Sam find in Ellen's folder?

39. What does the little boy see in the haunted house?

40. What kind of chair does Sam sit on?

41. True or false: Sam is having second thoughts about going back to college when they have killed the demon?

42. What job do Dean and Sam take at the circus – litter pickers, ticket sellers or roustabouts?

43. How do the brothers discover the clown isn't a spirit?

44. What kind of monster is the clown?

45. How do you kill it?

Episode 3 – Bloodlust

46. What happens to the first girl we see?

47. What song is playing as we see the Impala come onto screen?

48. True or false: The brothers pose as journalists?

49. What do Dean and Sam find in the victim's mouth?

50. Who do the brothers meet in the bar?

51. How long has the above been tracking the vampire nest?

52. How did Gordon get into hunting?

53. True or false: Gordon confesses to killing his sister?

54. What is Ellen's advice to Sam?

55. What happens to Sam at the motel?

56. What is different about this nest of vampires – they only kill those who deserve it, they live off animal blood or they feed on the newly dead?

57. What is the name of the female vampire Gordon tortures?

58. What does Gordon cover his knife in?

59. How does Gordon try and make his point?

60. What do Dean and Sam do to Gordon?

Jensen Ackles (Dean Winchester) and Jared Padalecki (Sam Winchester)

'Our job is hunting evil. And if these things aren't killing people, they're not evil!' ~ Sam Winchester

61. Jensen Ackles modelled for which two magazines in 2006 and 2007?

62. Jared Padalecki wasn't able to attend the first *Supernatural* convention in the UK, Asylum 2007, because he was filming which 2008 movie?

63. What pet name does Jensen Ackles' character, Dean, sometimes call his brother, Sam, in *Supernatural*?

64. Jensen Ackles has an older brother and a younger sister, can you name them?

65. In 2007 Jared was nominated for the Teen Choice Award for 'TV Actor Drama' for his role as Sam Winchester in *Supernatural*, what English actor did he lose out to?

66. Jared was also nominated for the above award in 2002, for his role in which American TV series?

67. True or false: There is a town called Dean, near Winchester in Southampton, in the UK?

68. What American sci-fi TV series did Jensen appear in 2001-2002?

69. What powers does Sam Winchester possess as one of the Yellow-eyed demon's 'special children'?

70. Jensen was nominated for 'Best Male Performance in a 2006 Science Fiction Television Episode' at the Canadian Constellation Awards, for which episode of *Supernatural* Season 2?

71. How is Jensen's dad, Alan Ackles, affectionately
     referred to by the *Supernatural* fandom?

72. What American reality TV series did Jared
     Padalecki host during July and August 2007?

73. What is Dean Winchester's job in his dream world
     in episode 20 'What Is and What Should Never Be'?

74. Jared Padalecki was executive producer on the first
     album of which band in 2007?

75. True or false: Jared directed two episodes of
     Supernatural Season 2?

Episode 4 – Children Shouldn't Play With Dead Things

76. What happens to Angela Mason?

77. What does Sam want to visit?

78. What does Dean notice in the graveyard that is unusual?

79. What is Angela's father's profession?

80. What happens to plants wherever the spirit goes?

81. Who does Dean tell Angela's roommate he is?

82. What is Angela's boyfriend called – Mark, Malcolm or Matt?

83. What do the police think happened to him?

84. What do Dean and Sam find on the inside of Angela's coffin?

85. Neil was Angela's best friend, why does Dean suspect that he brought Angela back from the dead?

86. Who else does Angela attack other than Matt?

87. Why?

88. What has Neil turned Angela into – a werewolf, a zombie or a vengeful spirit?

89. How do Dean and Sam kill Angela?

90. Which movie adapted from the novel by Stephen King is referenced in this episode?

Episode 5 – Simon Said

91. What happens in the first scene?

92. What is unusual about the way 'doc' kills Dennis and himself?

93. What do we discover the first scene is – a dream, a flashback or a premonition?

94. Who do Dean and Sam go to visit at the Roundhouse?

95. What does Sam ask Ash to look up?

96. What does the waitress say to look out for?

97. What prized possession does Dean give to Andy and why?

98. What does Dean say he thinks is going on?

99. What does the 'doc' from the first scene do after Sam sets off the alarm in the gun shop?

100. Why does Andy's mind control not work on Sam?

101. What is Sam's next vision?

102. Who is the woman?

103. True or false: Andy has an 'evil' twin?

104. Who has Andy's twin been posing as?

105. Who appears to Andy's twin in a dream?

Supernatural Quotes

*'Something big is going down – end-of-the
world big.' ~ Bobby Singer*

106. Which episode in Season 2 features the famous lines 'You talking to me? Are you talking to me?' immortalised by Robert De Niro in the movie *Taxi Driver*?

107. What Season 2 character describes his hair as 'All business up front, party in the back'?

108. Who is Sam with in episode 17 when Dean phones him and says: 'Let me guess. You're sitting on the couch like a stiff, thinking of something to say.'?

109. Who asks Professor Arthur Cox: 'Don't you like me anymore, don't you want me?' in episode 15 'Tall Tales'?

110. Who tells Dean, 'You're not the first soldier I've plucked from the field,' in episode 1 'In My Time of Dying'?

111. Who says the following to John Winchester in episode 1 'In My Time of Dying': 'I took you for a lot of things. But suicidally reckless wasn't one of them.'?

112. Who says: 'Careful now, wouldn't want to damage this fine packaging' in episode 14 'Born Under a Bad Sign' – Dean or Sam?

113. What character describes Dean as 'One hell of a PA' in episode 18 'Hollywood Babylon'?

114. In episode 13 'Houses of the Holy' what character asks, 'You mean am I stark-raving crazy for coca puffs' – Gaynor, Gloria or Gale?

115. Complete the quote by the crossroads demon (episode 22 'All Hell Breaks Loose: Part Two'): 'And because I'm such a saint, I'll give you one year...'

116. Who tells Sam to 'lighten up a little' in episode 3 'Bloodlust', also calling him 'Sammy'?

117. Who accuses Dean and Sam of 'bickering like an old married couple' in episode 15 'Tall Tales'?

118. What character describes themself as a 'freak with a knife collection' in episode 6 'No Exit'?

119. In episode 18 'Hollywood Babylon' who says 'Now that's what I'm talking about'?

120. Complete the quote from episode 14 'Born Under a Bad Sign': 'Don't try to con...'

Episode 6 – No Exit

121. What is the girl complaining about on the phone?

122. What starts oozing from the walls and ceilings?

123. Who has picked up the case?

124. How do they pay for the apartment?

125. What is the spirit's 'type' of victim?

126. What do Dean and Jo find in the vent – human skin, blonde hair or human remains?

127. Who owns Jo's knife before she does?

128. What particular smell does Jo recall about her dad?

129. What do Dean, Sam and Jo discover about the building next door?

130. Who has been locked up in the prison?

131. What does Sam discover under the building?

132. What do Dean and Sam use to find the underground sewage works?

133. True or false: The girl that the spirit has kept alive is called Tessa?

134. Who do Dean and Sam use as bait to trap the spirit?

135. What does Ellen tell Jo about her dad's death?

Episode 7 – The Usual Suspects

136. Can you list the things Dean is arrested for?

137. What is Sam's excuse for 'falling off the map'?

138. What word has been typed out over and over again?

139. How long does Sam say it will take to crack the password – 15 minutes, 30 minutes or 45 minutes?

140. Why do the police think Dean is the murderer?

141. What type of lawyer is Tony Giles?

142. What famous lines does Dean say whilst 'confessing'?

143. What does Dean think 'danashulps' stands for?

144. What movie does Sam emulate when making his escape?

145. What does the detective witness in the bathroom?

146. What does the above have on her wrists?

147. Where do the letters 'sup' from 'danashulps', come from?

148. What do Sam and Detective Diana Ballard discover around the victim, Claire's neck?

149. Who is responsible for Claire's murder?

150. True or false: Detective Diana Ballard lets Dean and Sam go, so that they can continue hunting the supernatural?

Cast and Crew

*'I come in from a character's point of view, it's
all about characters to me and I let the plot work
itself out...' ~ Robert Singer, Director*

151. What actress plays the part of the reaper, Tessa, in
episode 1 'In My Time of Dying'?

152. How many episodes of *Supernatural* Season 2 were
directed by Kim Manners – four, five or six?

153. What writer and producer wrote four episodes of
Season 2, including episode 9 'Croatoan'?

154. What actor plays the role of Ash in *Supernatural*
Season 2?

155. What character is played by David Monahan in
episode 13 'Houses of the Holy'?

156. Can you name the regular director of *Supernatural*
who directed episode 2 'Everybody Loves a Clown',
episode 12 'Nightshifter' and episode 18
'Hollywood Babylon'?

157. What character does Sterling K. Brown play in
Supernatural Season 2?

158. Which 1973 cult supernatural horror movie did
actress Linda Blair, who plays Detective Diana
Ballard in episode 7 'The Usual Suspects', appear
in?

159. How many episodes of *Supernatural* Season 2 were
written by Sera Gamble?

160. Actor Charles Malik Whitfield plays the role of Victor Henrikson in episode 12 'Nightshifter' and episode 19 'Folsom Prison Blues', but what is his onscreen job?

161. What actor plays the Trickster in episode 15 'Tall Tales'?

162. What character is played by Gabriel Tigerman in *Supernatural* Season 2?

163. True or false: Writer Raelle Tucker left *Supernatural* at the end of Season 2 to work on *True Blood*?

164. What actor plays the role of Robert Johnson in episode 8 'Crossroad Blues'?

165. Can you name the *Saw II* actress who plays Madison in episode 17 'Heart'?

Episode 8 – Crossroad Blues

166. What does the musician start hearing?

167. What is Robert Johnson saying as he dies?

168. What does the receptionist give Dean that he is confused about?

169. What bar had both the architect and Miss Pearlman visited ten years ago?

170. What does Miss Pearlman think she sees?

171. What flowers are growing at the crossroad by Lloyds Bar?

172. Why are they significant?

173. What do Dean and Sam discover after digging in the centre of the crossroad?

174. What are crossroads used for?

175. What animals are attacking the people who made deals – werewolves, hellhounds or devil dogs?

176. How do you seal a deal with a demon at the crossroad?

177. What does George Darrow have underneath his door – goofer dust, rock salt or iron rods?

178. Why did Evan Hudson make a deal?

179. What do Dean and Sam plan to do with the crossroads demon?

180. True or false: Dean makes a deal with the crossroads demon?

Episode 9 – Croatoan

181. The first scene we see is another of Sam's visions, what happens?

182. What does the man have tattooed on his arm?

183. What does it signify?

184. How does Dean know this?

185. What Company was John Winchester in?

186. What word is carved into the signpost that Sam walks into?

187. Where do the brothers take Mrs Tanner (Beverly) after they rescue her from her husband and son – the hospital, the doctor's surgery or the church?

188. How does Mrs Tanner describe her husband and son's uncharacteristic behaviour?

189. What does Dean come across whilst driving to the next town?

190. What three things does the doctor find in Mr Tanner's blood results?

191. When Dean arrives at the bridge, what does he find?

192. What is the reason for this?

193. What does Sam find in John's journal about Croatoan?

194. On the way back, who does Dean run into?

195. What does Hannah do to Sam?

Samantha Ferris (Ellen Harvelle)

'...something big and bad's coming and it's coming fast, and their side holds all the cards.'

196. What nationality is Samantha – American, Canadian or Australian?

197. Can you name the romantic comedy film that Samantha appeared in 2006?

198. In what year was Samantha born?

199. What first name did Samantha Ferris go by when she worked as a television reporter prior to becoming an actress?

200. Samantha played Diane in the 2007 crime thriller *Butterfly on a Wheel* alongside which James Bond actor?

201. What is the first episode that Samantha's character, Ellen Harvelle, appears in *Supernatural*?

202. Who described Samantha's *Supernatural* character as a 'gun-toting, beer-slinging, bar-owning broad'?

203. Samantha is known to be an animal lover, what does she have as a pet – a snake, a cat or a tarantula?

204. In what year did Samantha appear in the TV series *Battlestar Gallactica* in an episode titled 'Dirty Hands'?

205. What is the relationship between Ellen (Samantha Ferris) and Jo Harvelle (Alona Tal) in *Supernatural*?

206. For what PS2 game did Samantha provide one of the voices in 2005?

207. What three things does Samantha have a fear of?

208. What sporting occupation did Samantha aspire to as
a child?

209. Samantha appeared as Lt. Alexa Brenner in seven
episodes of which TV series in 2006?

210. True or false: Samantha was a weathergirl on a local
TV station during the 1990s?

Episode 10 – Hunted

211. What ability does the boy in the first scene (Scott Carey) have?

212. Who appears in his dreams?

213. What did John say to Dean before he died?

214. Who dreams about Sam getting blown up?

215. Who else's death does the above see in a vision?

216. Who tells Dean where to find Sam?

217. What has happened to Jo Harvelle – she has been possessed by a demon, kidnapped by Gordon Walker or run away to become a hunter?

218. How does Sam get Scott's confidential files and voice recording from the psychologist?

219. Who shoots at Sam and Ava Wilson?

220. What does Sam learn from the bullet he finds?

221. What are Dean and Sam's code words for 'there's a gun at my head'?

222. What is the name of the street, the same as the surname of a famous American actress, where Gordon is keeping Dean hostage?

223. Why does Gordon want to kill Sam?

224. What three things do Dean and Sam discover at Ava's house?

225. Who goes missing at the end of the episode?

Episode 11 – Playthings

226. What happens to the dolls in the dolls' house?

227. Who is the person on the missing person's poster?

228. What does Sam say happened to the first victim in the hotel?

229. How long have Dean and Sam been looking for Ava – one week, one month or one year?

230. Who does Dean say they may run into inside the hotel and what TV show are they from?

231. What does Sam find outside on a flowerpot?

232. What does the hotel owner, Susan, tell Dean and Sam about the hotel?

233. What is the connection between the two victims?

234. Who do the dolls/Tyler's toys belong to?

235. What does Sam make Dean promise him?

236. Who do they think taught Rose Hoodoo?

237. What happens to the things in the playground outside (and in the dolls' house)?

238. What is actually happening in the house?

239. Why was Rose using Hoodoo magic?

240. Who is Tyler's imaginary friend and what does she do to Tyler?

Alona Tal (Jo Harvelle)

*'Scream all you want… but there's no way you're
stepping over that salt!'*

241. In what country was Alona born?

242. To what US city did Alona move to when she left
her home country?

243. What musician and actor did Alona record a song
with in 2003?

244. In what year was Alona born – 1981, 1983 or 1985?

245. Alona married which actor, known for his
appearances in *Pacific Blue*, in June 2007?

246. In which American action movie, released on video,
did Alona play Ellie Burke in 2007?

247. According to her Twitter page (@atalalona) where
does Alona live?

248. In what 2007 movie did Alona play the lead role,
Devon Thompson?

249. How many episodes of the 2007 American TV
drama *Cane* did Alona appear in?

250. Alona appeared in ten episodes of the American TV
series *Veronica Mars* in 2004-5, what was the
character she played?

251. True or false: Alona appeared at Asylum, the first
Supernatural convention held in the UK, in 2007?

252. What is the middle name of the character Alona
plays in *Supernatural*, Jo Harvelle?

253. Jo Harvelle makes her first appearance in
Supernatural in Season 2 episode 2 'Everybody
Loves a Clown', in what month and year was this
episode first aired?

254. In which episode of Season 2 does Alona's
character, Jo Harvelle, discover the truth about how
her father died?

255. What 1960s and '70s movie actor does Jo Harvelle
compare her dad to in episode 6 'No Exit'?

Episode 12 – Nightshifter

256. What bank was being robbed at the beginning of the episode – Bank of New Orleans, City Bank of Milwaukee or Boston National Bank?

257. Who comes out of the bank with a hostage?

258. What happens at the jewellery shop?

259. Who do the Winchesters go and see with the initials 'RR'?

260. What is Ronald's eyewitness account of the incidents?

261. What do the security tapes show?

262. What monster are Dean and Sam hunting?

263. Where do the above creatures like to hide?

264. True or false: Ronald chains the doors to the bank and starts shooting at the ceiling?

265. What does Ronald slip on?

266. What do the police do to the bank?

267. What does Dean find in the ceiling – shapeshifter skin, a dead body or a stash of guns?

268. Who shoots Ronald?

269. Who does the shapeshifter turn into?

270. What do Dean and Sam disguise themselves as to escape from the bank?

Episode 13 – Houses of the Holy

271. Which one of the Winchester brothers is looking after Gloria in the psychiatric hospital, Dean or Sam?

272. Why is Gloria in the hospital?

273. Who does she say God sent to talk to her?

274. What is Dean doing when Sam walks into the hotel room?

275. True or false: Dean says that angels don't exist?

276. What does Gloria say the angel gave her?

277. What do Dean and Sam find in Gully's basement?

278. What does Sam find on the next victim's computer?

279. What is the link between the two victims?

280. Who is the memorial on the church steps for?

281. What has the priest been praying for?

282. What does Sam see when he and Dean are in the crypt?

283. What plant is growing on Gregory's grave – ivy, wormwood or nettles?

284. Who or what does the 'angel' turn out to be?

285. What changes Dean's view on religion and the existence of angels?

Supernatural Soundtrack

286. The music of which African-American blues singer,
who according to legend sold his soul to the devil in
exchange for his talent, features in episode 8
'Crossroad Blues'?

287. What track by American pop duo Captain &
Tennille is playing in the van that Dean and Sam
drive to Harvelle's Roadhouse in episode 2
'Everybody Loves a Clown'?

288. What is the closing track that plays when Dean and
Sam are at the Roadhouse with Ellen at the end of
episode 5 'Simon Said'?

289. In episode 12 'Nightshifter' the song 'Renegade'
plays at the end when the brothers drive away in
SWAT uniforms, but what American rock band
recorded the track?

290. What song is playing in episode 15 'Tall Tales'
when the fratboy is dancing with the alien?

291. Which Season 2 episode features the song 'Voodoo
Spell' by Michael Burkes?

292. What song by British-American rock band Foreigner
is playing in the car when Dean and Sam drive Ellen
and Jo home in episode 6 'No Exit' – 'Urgent',
'Cold as Ice' or 'Hot Blooded'?

293. Where is Dean in episode 17 'Heart' when
'Smoking Gun' by Kip Winger is playing?

294. Which food-related song by Booker T. & the M.G.s plays at the beginning of episode 19 'Folsom Prison Blues' when Dean and Sam go to jail?

295. In episode 1 'In My Time of Dying' what song plays immediately after the accident?

296. What Bob Dylan track plays at the end of episode 13 'Houses of the Holy'?

297. Which artist's version of 'What a Wonderful World' features on the soundtrack of episode 20 'What Is and What Never Should Be' – Louis Armstrong, Michael Bublé or Joey Ramone?

298. Which song by Frank Sinatra features on the soundtrack of episode 18 'Hollywood Babylon'?

299. Which Barry White song is playing when Dean enters the lecture theatre to confront the Trickster in episode 15 'Tall Tales'?

300. What is the last song played at the end of episode 22 'All Hell Breaks Loose: Part Two', the series finale?

Episode 14 – Born Under a Bad Sign

301. Who is Dean looking for at the beginning of the episode?

302. What does Sam have on his hands and shirt?

303. What can Sam remember about what happened?

304. What does Sam have in his pocket?

305. What do Dean and Sam find in the back seat of the car – a dead body, a vampire fang or a dagger?

306. What do the brothers discover at the house?

307. Who do Dean and Sam see on security footage killing the man?

308. What two emotions does Sam tell Dean he has been feeling over the past couple weeks?

309. Who do we see Sam meet up with?

310. What does Sam have on his arm – a tattoo, a burn mark or a knife wound?

311. What does Sam do to Jo?

312. What is wrong with Sam?

313. What does Bobby give Sam to drink?

314. How does Bobby get the demon out of Sam?

315. What does Bobby give to Dean and Sam?

Episode 15 – Tall Tales

316. What is the professor's name?

317. What does the girl turn into?

318. Who is there when the professor 'falls' out of the window?

319. What is he a professor of?

320. Can you name the shots Dean is drinking at the bar?

321. What happens to the next victim?

322. What did Curtis do with the alien – slow dance, play guitar or rap?

323. What belonging to Sam goes missing?

324. What word does Sam use to describe Dean's food?

325. What do all the 'victims' have in common?

326. What happens to the Impala?

327. What are Dean and Sam up against?

328. True or false: the above monster targets the high and mighty/people who need teaching a lesson?

329. What does the above monster like to eat?

330. True or false: Dean kills the Trickster at the end of the episode?

Fredric Lehne (Yellow-eyed demon)

'I'm looking for the best and brightest of your generation.'

331. In what year was Fredric Lehne born – 1959, 1960 or 1961?

332. Fredric made his Broadway debut at the age of 21 in which play by Ibsen?

333. What other surname does Fredric sometimes go by as an actor?

334. What American television series did Fredric appear in as Mr Carver in 2005?

335. What role did Fredric play in the TV series *The Book of Daniel*?

336. Can you name Fredric's wife who shares her Christian name with a well-known 20th century American dancer and actress?

337. In what American TV series did Fredric play Eugene 'Topper' Barnes in 2007?

338. True or false: Fredric has appeared in *CSI: Crime Scene Investigation?*

339. What long-running popular American TV series did Fredric appear in from 2004-2010?

340. What cult 1997 movie did Fredric appear in as Agent Janus?

341. By what nickname, derived from a popular singer, is the Yellow-eyed demon sometimes referred to by fans?

342. True or false: The Yellow-eyed demon can possess
reapers as well as humans?

343. In what episode of Season 2 does the Yellow-eyed
demon first appear?

344. Which character sets up a tracking system to alert
Dean and Sam of Yellow-eyes' whereabouts in
episode 2 'Everybody Loves a Clown'?

345. Name three things that can stop the Yellow-eyed
demon?

Episode 16 – Roadkill

346. What happens to the couple in the first scene?

347. What does Molly discover whilst looking for her husband?

348. Who is in the cabin?

349. What is wrong with Jonah Greely?

350. Who does Molly flag down to help her?

351. As they are driving the radio changes and plays what song?

352. What do the brothers and Molly find in the cabin?

353. What do they discover about Jonah?

354. What does Dean find in the house?

355. What do they find through the door?

356. What device starts playing the song again?

357. What is written on the window in frost/ice?

358. Where does Sam think the man is buried – in the basement, under an old tree or in the local cemetery?

359. What does Molly discover about her husband, David?

360. What does Molly find out about herself?

Episode 17 – Heart

361. How does Nate get home – in a cab, his assistant, Madison, gives him a lift or he walks?

362. What does the doctor think killed Nate?

363. What organ is missing from his body?

364. When are the murders taking place?

365. Dean and Sam pose as detectives Landis and Dante, what is the significance of these names?

366. Who has been stalking Madison?

367. What do Dean and Sam discover outside of the apartment belonging to Maddy's ex-boyfriend?

368. Who stays with Madison, to protect her, Dean or Sam?

369. What does Madison tell Sam had happened to her that had changed her life?

370. Who is the werewolf's next victim?

371. Dean discovers the true identity of the werewolf, who is it?

372. How long ago was Madison attacked?

373. Dean kills the werewolf who attacked Madison, who is it?

374. True or false: Dean and Sam succeed in finding a 'cure' for Madison?

375. How does Madison die?

Hunting Monsters (From Seasons 1 and 2)

'Our kind is practically extinct. Turns out we weren't quite as high up the food chain as we imagined.' ~ Lenore, vampire

376. How do you kill a werewolf?

377. What metal is used to repel spirits?

378. How do you kill a rakshasa?

379. What substance can paralyse a vampire?

380. How do you kill a wendigo?

381. When is the only time you can hurt or kill a shtriga?

382. Name three ways to kill a zombie?

383. What do you use to kill a djinn?

384. True or false: A reaper can be bound by a spell?

385. What kind of monster is appeased by human sacrifice?

386. What is used to banish a daeva?

387. How do you get rid of a ghost permanently?

388. How do you kill a shapeshifter?

389. To kill a trickster, you plunge a stake into its heart, dipped in what?

390. How do you catch a demon?

Episode 18 – Hollywood Babylon

391. Where is this episode set?

392. Who believes that the set is haunted?

393. What grisly sight does the lead actress, Tara, find?

394. What programme, starring Jared Padalecki, was also filmed on the *Hellhazers* set?

395. Why do the brothers go to Los Angeles?

396. What observation does Sam make about the weather?

397. Why are Dean and Sam on the movie set?

398. Brad mistakes Dean for a PA, what does he ask Dean to get him – a Hershey bar, a smoothie or fried chicken?

399. Dean tells Tara that he loved her performance in *Boogeyman*, what connection does this movie have to *Supernatural*?

400. True or false: To pass time on set Tara draws sketches of the cast?

401. Why did Frank fake his death?

402. What image appears to Brad?

403. Who is she?

404. How does producer Jay Wiley die?

405. Who is responsible for writing a summoning ritual into the script?

Episode 19 – Folsom Prison Blues

406. What sign of a ghostly presence occurs when the workmen open the cell door in the opening sequence?

407. What happens to the guard, Randall?

408. Who gets arrested for breaking and entering?

409. Can you list the many charges against Dean?

410. What colour is the prison uniform – yellow, black and white or orange?

411. How many people have died in the Green River County Detention Center prior to Dean and Sam's incarceration?

412. True or false: Dean and Sam got arrested on purpose?

413. What is the name of the inmate Dean picks a fight with?

414. How did notorious prison inmate Mark Moody die?

415. What does Sam steal from the kitchen?

416. What is the name of the ghostly nurse that appears to Dean and tries to kill him – Daphne, Delphine or Dolores?

417. Who helps Dean and Sam escape from prison?

418. Dean and Sam's lawyer, Mara Daniels, attempts to put the police off the scent, by sending them where?

419. Does nurse Glockner succeed in killing Deacon
     Kaylor and why?

420. The brothers need to go 'deep' undercover for a
     while, where does Sam suggest?

Monsters and Spirits – Origins and Traits

421. What is the origin of a rakshasa?

422. In episode 4 'Children Shouldn't Play With Dead
Things' Dean and Sam encounter their first Zombie,
how was she reanimated?

423. How do hellhounds choose their victims?

424. The zombies in episode 9 'Croatoan' are infected by
a particular virus passed on how?

425. Where does the word 'werewolf' originate from?

426. What creature is said to have been created by Allah
from a smokeless fire and existed before mankind?

427. What kind of demon disguises itself as a little girl?

428. How is a vengeful spirit created?

429. A reaper's role is to escort the souls of the deceased
to the afterlife. The dead can refuse to accompany a
reaper and, if so, what fate awaits them?

430. Famous tricksters include Mercurius from Roman
mythology, Loki from Norse mythology and Anansi
from West African folklore, what is the trickster
from Greek mythology called?

431. True or false: A vampire can survive on animal
blood and does not have to feed on humans?

432. Apart from vampires, what other *Supernatural*
Season 2 monster feeds on human blood?

433. According to popular folklore, how can you 'cure' a werewolf?

434. What is ectoplasm?

435. What substance denotes the presence of demons?

Episode 20 – What Is and What Should Never Be

436. What is Dean hunting at the start of the episode?

437. What is Dean's imaginary girlfriend called – Carmen, Carmel or Carol?

438. What did Dean see after visiting the college?

439. In Dean's imaginary world who does Sam arrive at their mother's house with?

440. What surprise do the couple have for Dean?

441. What is it the anniversary of?

442. Whilst hallucinating, what does Dean find hanging in his closet?

443. Whose grave does Dean visit?

444. What does Dean attempt to steal from his mother's house?

445. True or false: Sam finds a jar of lamb's blood in Dean's car?

446. What does Dean do when Sam tries ringing for help?

447. Who is the djinn keeping captive?

448. What is the djinn doing to his prisoner?

449. What does Dean do to get back to reality?

450. Who is with Dean when he wakes up?

Episode 21 – All Hell Breaks Loose: Part One

451. What happens whilst Dean is waiting in the car for Sam that concerns him?

452. What does Dean discover when he enters the diner?

453. Where does Sam wake up?

454. Who jumps out at Sam?

455. How does Andy describe the ghost town?

456. Who does Sam discover locked in a shed?

457. Who else is with them in the deserted town?

458. Dean and Bobby are trying to find out where Sam has been taken, who rings Dean with information – Ash, Ellen or Bobby?

459. Who attacks Jake?

460. What does Sam find engraved on an old bell and what does he remember about the town?

461. What do Dean and Bobby discover has happened to Harvelle's Roadhouse?

462. Who do Sam and the others discover hanging from the water vane?

463. Who appears to Sam in his dream?

464. What does he show Sam?

465. True or false: Sam is stabbed by Jake and dies at the end of the episode?

Episode 22 – All Hell Breaks Loose: Part Two

466. At the beginning of the episode what does Bobby suggest to Dean that they do with Sam?

467. Who appears to Jake and what does he tell him?

468. Why is Dean so distraught?

469. Who does Dean summon?

470. How long does the demon offer Dean in return for Sam's life – one year, five years or ten years?

471. What does Dean tell Sam happened to him?

472. According to Bobby, what demonic omens had suddenly increased?

473. Who do Dean and Bobby find in the car lot?

474. What has Ash left in the safe at the Roadhouse?

475. What do the Xs mark?

476. What connects the churches

477. True or false: The crypt is a door to hell?

478. Who opens the door with the Colt?

479. Who climbs out of hell to help Dean and Sam

480. Who shoots the Yellow-eyed demon with the Colt, Dean or Sam?

Supernatural Trivia

*'There are non-parametrics, statistical
overviews, prospects and correlations, I mean...
damn! They're signs. Omens.' ~ Ash*

481. *Supernatural* is largely filmed on location where?

482. What is the Inn at the beginning of episode 11 'Playthings' called?

483. In episode 10 'Hunted' Gordon refers to 'Mr Tinkles the cat', what 2001 film does Mr Tinkles feature in?

484. What two 'escape' movies are referenced in episode 19 'Folsom Prison Blues'?

485. When Sam checks into a hotel in episode 14 'Born Under a bad Sign' what name does he use?

486. The reaper, Tessa, in episode 1 'In My Time of Dying' is similar to the character 'Death' from which comic book series by writer Neil Gaiman?

487. Why is Jared Padalecki seen wearing a cast on his arm from episode 5 'Simon Said' to episode 11 'Playthings'?

488. What eye colour denotes a crossroads demon?

489. 'We're not in Kansas anymore' and 'Aunty Em, there's no place like home' in episode 20 'What Is and What Should Never Be' are famous lines from which film?

490. In episode 21 'All Hell Breaks Loose: Part One' Dean uses the signature of which *Baywatch* actor?

491. What game do Dean and Sam play to decide which one of them will do something, in episode 17 'Heart' and throughout the series?

492. Clif Kosterman is a bodyguard and driver for Jared
Padalecki and Jensen Ackles, what role did he play
in Season 2 episode 19 'Folsom Prison Blues'?

493. Episode 2 'Everybody Loves a Clown' features a
rakshasa, what 1970s American TV science
fiction/supernatural drama also featured this
creature?

494. In episode 15 'Tall Tales', Dean is drinking Purple
Nurples, a real cocktail made up of what?

495. What famous, real life, bank robbing duo are
referred to in episode 12 'Nightshifter'?

496. Elizabeth Stride, whose image is depicted in episode
6 'No Exit' was a victim of which English serial
killer?

497. Episode 11 'Playthings' is set in an Inn in Cornwall,
Connecticut but what ghostly claim to fame does the
town also have?

498. The town, Sidewinder, referred to episode 9
'Croatoan' comes from which 1980 movie?

499. So that they can find one another, if separated, Dean
and Sam Winchester check into the first motel in the
phone book and sign in as what character from a
1970s American detective TV drama?

500. What are the last words, spoken by Dean, in
Supernatural Season 2?

Answers

Episode 1 – In My Time of Dying

1. Sam Winchester

2. It is empty

3. She can't see or hear him

4. His physical body (in a coma)

5. That he is awake

6. That he may not wake up

7. 'Come on Sam, go find some Hoodoo priest to lay some mojo on me'

8. Fetch the Colt from the Impala and get some other items to repel the demon

9. That you use the listed items to *summon* a demon

10. Knocks a glass of the table

11. A ghostly presence

12. A girl called Tessa

13. Through a ouija board

14. A reaper, she has come to reap his soul

15. He makes a deal with the Yellow-eyed demon: Dean's life in exchange for the Colt and his soul

Episode Titles

16. Episode 6 'No Exit'

17. Led Zeppelin

18. Episode 18 'Hollywood Babylon'

19. Robert Johnson

20. Episode 14 'Born Under a Bad Sign'

21. Bob Clark

22. Episode 1 'In My Time of Dying'

23. Gary Lewis & the Playboys

24. Episode 19 'Folsom Prison Blues'

25. A movie (1961)

26. Episode 7 'The Usual Suspects'

27. Roanaoke (the Lost Colony)

28. Episode 5 'Simon Said' (Simon Says)

29. Led Zeppelin

30. Episodes 21 and 22 'All Hell Breaks Loose: Parts One and Two'

Episode 2 – Everybody Loves a Clown

31. A clown (she saw at the fair earlier)

32. Outside her window at home

33. Kills them

34. Their father's, John Winchester

35. A voicemail from a woman called Ellen

36. Harvelle's Roadhouse

37. Ellen Harvelle; her daughter, Jo Harvelle; and Ash, a Roadhouse regular

38. Information about a possible hunt involving multiple murders

39. The clown

40. A chair shaped like a clown (he has a phobia of clowns)

41. True

42. Litter pickers

43. Rock salt has no effect on it

44. A Rakshasa

45. With a dagger made of pure brass

Episode 3 – Bloodlust

46. Her head gets cut off

47. 'Back in Black' by AC/DC

48. True

49. Vampire fangs

50. Gordon Walker, a hunter

51. A year

52. A vampire took his sister

53. True

54. Leave Gordon to it and move on

55. The vampires find him

56. They live off of animal blood (and never kill humans)

57. Lenore

58. Dead man's blood

59. He cuts open Sam's arm and drips his blood into the vampire's mouth

60. They tie him up and leave him

Jensen Ackles (Dean Winchester) and Jared Padalecki (Sam Winchester)

61. *Men's Fitness* (October 2006) and *Hollywood Life* (June 2007)

62. *The Christmas Cottage* (renamed *Thomas Kinkade's Christmas Cottage*)

63. Sammy

64. Joshua and Mackenzie

65. Hugh Laurie (for his role in *House*)

66. *Gilmore Girls*

67. True

68. *Dark Angel* (22 episodes as Ben X5-493 and Alec X5-494)

69. Premonitions and telekinesis

70. Episode 1 'In My Time of Dying'

71. Papa Ackles

72. *Room 401*

73. Mechanic

74. Brian Buckley Band (album: 'For Her')

75. False: Jared didn't direct any of the episodes

Episode 4 – Children Shouldn't Play With Dead Things

76. She dies in a car accident

77. Their mother's grave

78. A perfect circle of dead grass (around Angela Mason's *newly dug* grave)

79. A professor who teaches Ancient Greek

80. They die

81. Angela's cousin, Alan Stanwig

82. Matt (Harrison)

83. That he slit his own throat (committed suicide)

84. Ancient Greek Symbols that are used for necromancy and communicating with the dead (but no human remains)

85. Dean reads in Angela's diary that Neil was not only her friend, but also her father's assistant, meaning he had access to books on Ancient Greece

86. Her roommate, Lindsey

87. She wants revenge after finding out that Matt and Lindsey had slept together before she died

88. A zombie

89. By tricking her back to her grave and stabbing her with a silver stake

90. *Pet Sematary*

Episode 5 – Simon Said

91. A man walks into a shop, shoots the owner, Dennis, and himself

92. How calm he is although he says 'guns make him nervous'

93. A premonition

94. Ash (aka 'Dr Badass', according to the sign on his door)

95. A house fire in 1983, the baby's nursery, night of the child's six month birthday

96. A van with a barbarian queen, riding a polar bear, painted on the side of it

97. His Impala, because Andy asks if he can have it

98. Mind control

99. He walks out in front of a bus

100. Because Sam is psychic too

101. A woman covering herself in petrol and setting herself on fire

102. Holly Becket, Andy's biological mother

103. True

104. Andy's friend and a waiter at the diner

105. The Yellow-eyed demon

106. Episode 19 'Folsom Prison Blues' spoken by Lucas when Dean picks a fight with him

107. Ash (episode 2 'Everybody Loves a Clown')

108. Madison (the werewolf)

109. The decomposing ghost of a once-attractive girl

110. Tessa (a reaper)

111. The Yellow-eyed demon

112. Sam Winchester (when he is possessed by a demon)

113. Tara Benchley (horror movie actress)

114. Gloria

115. 'And one year only.'

116. Gordon Walker

117. Bobby Singer

118. Jo Harvelle

119. The director of *Hellhazers II* (when Tara screams after discovering the body of a stage-hand hanging from the rafters)

120. A con man

Episode 6 – No Exit

121. Faulty wiring

122. Black ectoplasm

123. Jo Harvelle (Ellen's daughter)

124. Jo has the money from playing poker

125. Young, blonde females

126. Blonde hair

127. Her father, William Antony Harvelle

128. The smell of his old leather jacket when he came home from hunts

129. It is an old prison

130. H H Holmes (Herman Webster Mudgett, aka Dr Henry Howard Holmes, America's first serial killer)

131. An old sewer system

132. A metal detector

133. False: Teresa

134. Jo Harvelle

135. John Winchester (Dean and Sam's father) was responsible

Episode 7 – The Usual Suspects

136. Credit card fraud, breaking and entering, grave desecration, torture and murder

137. He needed time 'to deal', so he is on a road trip with his brother

138. Danashulps

139. About 30 minutes

140. He is found at the crime scene with Karen's body

141. A defence lawyer

142. 'My name is Dean Winchester, I'm an Aquarius. I enjoy sunsets, long walks on the beach and frisky women.'

143. An anagram of a street name; Ashland

144. *The Great Escape* (method used by Hilts)

145. The taps turning themselves on, wording on the mirror and an angry woman appears with her throat slit (and a lot of blood)

146. Strange bruising, possibly from a rope

147. The wording on the window of the building where Claire's body is located (Ashland sup – an anagram of 'danashulps')

148. The same necklace that Diana, the detective, has around her neck

149. The police officer, Pete Sheridan

150. True

Cast and Crew

151. Lindsey McKeon

152. Six: episode 1 'In My Time of Dying', episode 4 'Children Shouldn't Play With Dead Things, episode 6 'No Exit', episode 13 'Houses of the Holy', episode 17 'Heart' and episode 22 'All Hell Breaks Loose: Part Two'

153. John Shiban (he also wrote episode 2 'Everybody Loves a Clown', episode 15 'Tall Tales' and episode 19 'Folsom Prison Blues')

154. Chad Lindberg

155. Father Thomas Gregory

156. Philip Sgriccia

157. Gordon Walker (episode 3 'Bloodlust' and episode 10 'Hunted')

158. *The Exorcist*

159. Five: episode 3 'Bloodlust', episode 8 'Crossroad Blues', episode 13 'Houses of the Holy, episode 17 'Heart' and episode 21 'All Hell Breaks Loose: Part One'

160. FBI Special Agent

161. Richard Speight Jr

162. Andy Gallagher (episode 5 'Simon Said' and episode 21 'All Hell Breaks Loose: Part One')

163. True: Raelle wrote four episodes of *Supernatural* Season 2 (episode 4 'Children Shouldn't Play With Dead Things', episode 10 'Hunted', episode 16 'Roadkill' and episode 20 'What Is and What Should Never Be')

164. La Monde Byrd

165. Emmanuelle Vaugier

Episode 8 – Crossroad Blues

166. Dogs howling and growling

167. 'Black dogs'

168. Her Myspace address

169. Lloyds Bar

170. The landlord's face contorting

171. Yellow flowers called yero flowers

172. They can be used in summoning rituals

173. A small metallic box full of graveyard dirt and a black cat bone

174. Summoning a demon to make a deal

175. Hellhounds

176. With a kiss

177. Goofer dust –Voodoo mixture that keeps away hellhounds

178. To cure his wife of cancer

179. Summon it and perform an exorcism

180. True

Episode 9 – Croatoan

181. Dean shoots a man tied to a chair

182. A bulldog's head

183. That he is a Master Sergeant

184. John Winchester (Dean and Sam's father) was in the corps as a Corporal

185. Echo 2-1

186. Croatoan

187. To the doctor's surgery

188. Like they had the devil in them

189. A crashed car with blood all over the seats and a bloody knife

190. That his lymphocyte percentage is high, his body is fighting off a virus and a weird sulphur residue

191. Cars and men with guns blocking the way

192. The town up ahead is being quarantined

193. That it was possibly a demon's name, otherwise known as Diva or Rechef, a demon of plague and pestilence

194. The Sergeant (from Sam's vision)

195. Infect him with blood

Samantha Ferris (Ellen Harvelle)

196. Canadian

197. *Gray Matters*

198. 1968

199. Janie

200. Pierce Brosnan

201. 'Everybody Loves a Clown' (Season 2 episode 2)

202. Samantha Ferris

203. A cat (called Abby)

204. 2007

205. Mother and daughter

206. SSX on Tour

207. Spiders, needles and death

208. Professional freestyle skier

209. *The Evidence*

210. True

Episode 10 – Hunted

211. He can electrocute things by touching them

212. A yellow-eyed man

213. That Dean must save Sam and if he couldn't he would have to kill him

214. Ava Wilson

215. Scott's; he gets stabbed

216. Ellen (Harvelle)

217. Run away to become a hunter

218. Ava pretends to be in therapy whilst Sam sneaks in to find them

219. Gordon Walker

220. It's a 233 calibre and the rifle had a suppressor

221. Funky town

222. Monroe Street

223. Because of his (Sam's) psychic abilities

224. Her dead fiancé, her engagement ring and sulphur on the windowsill

225. Ava Wilson

Episode 11 – Playthings

226. They move and represent what happened in real life

227. Ava Wilson

228. She drowned in the bath tub

229. One month

230. Fred and Daphne, *Scooby-doo*

231. A five point symbol – used for Voodoo spells

232. That it is closing in a month

233. Both are involved in the shutting down of the hotel

234. Grandma Rose – the old lady in the attic

235. That if he (Sam) turns into something he is not (evil), Dean has to kill him

236. Her nanny, who had a voodoo necklace

237. They start moving by themselves

238. It is haunted by a spirit

239. To protect the house and people in it from the spirit

240. Maggie (Thompson) – she tries to drown Tyler in the swimming pool so that she will always have someone to play with

Alona Tal (Jo Harvelle)

241. Israel

242. New York

243. Wyclef Jean (Party to Damascas)

244. 1983

245. Marcos Ferraez

246. *Half Past Dead 2*

247. la la land

248. *Taking Five*

249. Thirteen

250. Meg Manning

251. True

252. Beth

253. October 2006 (5th)

254. Episode 6 'No Exit' (he was killed on a hunt with John Winchester)

255. Steve McQueen

Episode 12 – Nightshifter

256. City Bank of Milwaukee

257. Dean Winchester

258. A customer robs the jewellery shop and then shoots the security guard in the face

259. Ronald Resnik

260. They were committed by a monster – half man, half machine

261. The bank robber's eyes flare at the camera (he has 'laser eyes' as Ronald puts it)

262. A shapeshifter

263. Underground

264. True

265. Shapeshifter skin

266. Cut off the power

267. A dead body

268. A police sniper

269. Sherry (a dead girl)

270. Members of the SWAT team

Episode 13 – Houses of the Holy

271. Sam

272. She stabbed someone because it was 'God's will'

273. An angel

274. He is on a massage bed listening to music

275. True

276. A sign outside Gully's (the victim's) house

277. A dead body

278. A locked folder full of emails to a thirteen-year-old girl

279. They attended the same church (Our Lady of the Angels)

280. Father Gregory

281. For deliverance from the violence and bloodshed

282. A bright light: The same thing everyone else is seeing

283. Wormwood – a plant that grows on the graves of spirits that are not at rest

284. The spirit of Father Gregory

285. The fourth victim gets killed (by a pole) trying to get away (God's will)

Supernatural Soundtrack

286. Robert Johnson (1911-1938)

287. Do That to Me One More Time

288. 'Fell on Black Days' by Soundgarden

289. Styx

290. 'Lady in Red' by Chris de Burgh

291. Episode 11 'Playthings'

292. Cold as Ice

293. At a strip club

294. Green Onions

295. 'Bad Moon Rising' by Creedence Clearwater Revival

296. Knockin' on Heaven's Door

297. Joey Ramone

298. I've Got the World on a String

299. Can't Get Enough of Your Love, Babe

300. 'Don't Look Back' by Boston

Episode 14 – Born Under a Bad Sign

301. His brother, Sam

302. Blood

303. Nothing

304. A key to a locked garage (in the hotel/apartment)

305. A dagger (covered in blood)

306. A dead hunter (Steve Wandell)

307. Sam

308. Rage and hate (that gets worse and worse)

309. Jo Harvelle

310. A burn mark – a binding link

311. He knocks her out and ties her up – she is bait

312. He is possessed by a demon (Meg)

313. Beer containing Holy water

314. He burns Sam's arm and breaks the link

315. Charms to stop demons getting in

Episode 15 – Tall Tales

316. Arthur Cox

317. A ghost

318. The Trickster

319. Philosophy and Morality

320. Purple Nurples

321. He is abducted by aliens

322. Slow dance

323. His laptop

324. Darwinism

325. They have all done bad things

326. The tyres have been let down

327. A trickster

328. True

329. Candy and sweet stuff

330. False: The trickster 'tricks' them into believing they have killed him and escapes

Fredric Lehne (Yellow-eyed demon)

331. 1959

332. *John Gabriel Borkman*

333. Lane

334. *Night Stalker*

335. Police Officer

336. Ginger (actress: Ginger Rogers)

337. *The Closer*

338. True: As Curt Ritten in 2001 and Frank Carrow in 2009

339. *Lost*

340. *Men in Black*

341. Celine Demon (Celine Dion)

342. True: The Yellow-eyed demon possesses the reaper, Tessa, in episode 1 'In My Time of Dying' in order to save Dean

343. Episode 1 'In My Time of Dying'

344. Ash

345. Iron, a devil's trap and the Colt

Episode 16 – Roadkill

346. They swerve to miss a man in the middle of the road and hit a tree

347. A cabin in the woods

348. The man they had tried to avoid running over (Jonah Greeley)

349. His face is decaying

350. The Winchester brothers in the Impala

351. 'The House of the Rising Sun' by the Animals (the same song that was playing when the couple crashed)

352. Love notes and a poem written by Jonah

353. He was killed in a car accident

354. A secret door

355. Another room with a skeleton hanging from the ceiling (Jonah's wife)

356. An old radio

357. 'She's mine'

358. Under an old tree

359. That he is alive but married to another woman

360. That she is dead and has been haunting Highway 41 for fifteen years

Episode 17 – Heart

361. In a cab

362. A wolf (or a pit bull as there are no wolves in San Francisco)

363. His heart

364. During the week leading up to full moon

365. John Landis directed the film *An American Werewolf in London* (1981) and Joe Dante directed *The Howling* (also 1981)

366. Her ex-boyfriend, Kurt

367. Claw marks on the wall

368. Sam

369. She was mugged

370. Kurt (Madison's ex)

371. Madison

372. One month

373. Glen, Madison's neighbour

374. False: The 'cure' doesn't work

375. Sam shoots her (through the heart with a silver bullet)

Hunting Monsters (From Seasons 1 and 2)

376. With a silver bullet through the heart

377. Iron

378. With a brass dagger

379. Dead man's blood

380. With fire (burn it death)

381. When it is feeding

382. Decapitation, head shot, staking the body inside the coffin with silver

383. A silver knife dipped in lamb's blood

384. True

385. Vanir

386. Extreme light

387. Salt and burn the physical remains

388. A silver bullet or blade through the heart, decapitation

389. The blood of its victim

390. In a devil's trap (mystical symbol that immobilises a demon)

Episode 18 – Hollywood Babylon

391. On a movie set (*Hellhazers II*)

392. Frank, a stage-hand

393. Frank, hanging from the rafters (and a vanishing figure)

394. *Gilmore Girls*

395. For a vacation

396. 'It's practically Canadian'

397. Because it is believed to be haunted

398. A smoothie

399. It was also written by Eric Kripke

400. False: She takes (Polaroid) photos

401. He was hired by the producers to generate publicity for the movie

402. The ghostly figure of a woman

403. Elise Drummond, a young actress who hung herself after a film producer ended their relationship

404. He is sucked into a massive fan

405. Walter Dixon, the original screenwriter

Episode 19 – Folsom Prison Blues

406. Their breath freezes

407. His arm gets trapped in the metal gate and he is killed

408. Dean and Sam Winchester

409. Mail fraud, credit card fraud, grave desecration, armed robbery, kidnapping and three accounts of first degree murder

410. Orange

411. Four

412. True: They are asked to investigate by the prison warden, Deacon Kaylor, an old friend of their father, John Winchester

413. Tiny

414. He was beaten to death by guards

415. Salt

416. Dolores (Glockner)

417. Deacon (the prison warden)

418. To the wrong cemetery

419. No, because Dean and Sam burn her bones

420. The Yemen

421. A rakshasa comes from Hindu myth and is considered to be a demon of chaos. A rakshasa can change its form, become invisible and animate dead bodies.

422. Through Greek Necromancy

423. The victims have made a deal with a crossroad demon, their souls for something in return, for example wealth, health, ability or in exchange for the life of another

424. Through blood

425. Greek mythology; a man that can shapeshift into a wolf, usually at the time of a full moon. Also known as lycanthropy from the Greek word for wolf 'lykoi' and man 'anthropos'

426. Djinn

427. Acheri demon

428. When a spirit acts violently to avenge a wrongdoing done to them in life

429. They remain in the Veil as ghosts and go on to become vengeful spirits

430. Hermes

431. True

432. A djinn

433. By killing the sire; the werewolf who turned them

434. A form of spiritual energy that allows a ghost to
     materialise

435. Sulphur

Episode 20 – What Is and What Should Never Be

436. A djinn

437. Carmen (Porter)

438. A girl in a white dress stained with blood and dirt

439. Jessica Moore (his girlfriend who was murdered by the Yellow-eyed demon)

440. They announce their engagement

441. Flight 424, a plane that Dean and Sam saved

442. Corpses

443. John Winchester's

444. A silver knife

445. True

446. Throws his phone out of the car window

447. The girl in white that Dean keeps seeing

448. Drinking her blood

449. Stabs himself (an old wives tale says that if you're about to die in a dream, you'll wake up)

450. His brother, Sam

Episode 21 – All Hell Breaks Loose: Part One

451. The radio starts flickering on and off

452. Sam is missing, everyone inside is dead and there is sulphur on the back door

453. In a deserted town (Cold Oak, South Dakota)

454. Andy Gallagher (from episode 5 'Simon Said')

455. Frontierland (Disney theme park based on the Wild West)

456. Ava Wilson (from episode 10 'Hunted')

457. Jake Talley (a soldier who served in Afghanistan)) and Lily

458. Ash

459. A demon in the shape of a little girl (acheri demon)

460. An old oak tree (telling Sam that they are in Cold Oak); the town is so haunted that all the residents left

461. It has burned to the ground and Ash is dead (Ellen is missing)

462. Lily

463. The Yellow-eyed demon

464. A vision of the night Sam's mother died, the demon fed baby Sam with his blood

465. True

Episode 22 – All Hell Breaks Loose: Part Two

466. Bury him

467. The Yellow-eyed demon; that Jake is the strongest and he has a job for him

468. He feels that it is his job to protect Sam and he has failed

469. A crossroad demon

470. One year

471. That Jake stabbed him but Bobby 'patched him up'

472. Cattle deaths and lightning storms (in all but one area of Wyoming)

473. Ellen Harvelle

474. A map marked with Xs

475. An abandoned 19th century frontier church built by Samuel Colt

476. Private iron railway lines that together form a pentagram, forming a 100 square mile devil's trap with a cemetery in the centre

477. True: A Devil's Gate

478. Jake

479. John Winchester (their father)

480. Dean

481. Vancouver, Canada

482. Pierpont Inn

483. *Cats and Dogs*

484. *The Great Escape* and *Escape from Alcatraz*

485. Richard Sambora (lead guitarist Bon Jovi)

486. *Sandman*

487. Jared broke his wrist in real life

488. Red

489. *The Wizard of Oz*

490. Hasselhoff (David Hasselhoff)

491. Rock, paper, scissors

492. Tiny

493. *Kolchak: The Night Stalker*

494. Malibu coconut rum, Triple Sec, Blue Curacao and cranberry juice

495. Bonnie and Clyde

496. Jack the Ripper

497. Cornwall is home to the remains of an abandoned town, one of the most haunted sites in the USA

498. *The Shining*

499. Jim Rockford from *The Rockford Files*

500. 'Well, then... we got work to do'

'Hope to hell you boys are ready, 'cause the war has just begun.' ~ Bobby Singer

Also by

Light Bulb Quizzes

The Supernatural Quiz Book Season 1

Coming soon

The Supernatural Quiz Book Season 3

Follow Light Bulb Quizzes on

Twitter: @LightBulbQuiz
and
Tumblr: lightbulbquizzes.tumblr.com

For news, giveaways
and forthcoming projects

www.ingramcontent.com/pod-product-compliance
Lightning Source LLC
Chambersburg PA
CBHW020622120726
47905CB00003B/900